GLADIATORS NEVER BLINK

Books by the same author

The Battle of Baked Bean Alley
Dennis Dipp on Gilbert's Pond

For older readers

Ackford's Monster
Normal Nesbitt, the Abnormally Average Boy
To Trust a Soldier
You've Been Noodled!

GLADIATORS
NEVER BLINK

NICK WARBURTON
Illustrations by
GRAHAM PHILPOT

WALKER BOOKS
AND SUBSIDIARIES
LONDON • BOSTON • SYDNEY

For Georgina

First published 1999 by Walker Books Ltd
87 Vauxhall Walk, London SE11 5HJ

2 4 6 8 10 9 7 5 3 1

Text © 1999 Nick Warburton
Illustrations © 1999 Graham Philpot

This book has been typeset in Plantin.

Printed in England by Clays Ltd, St Ives plc

British Library Cataloguing in Publication Data
A catalogue record for this book
is available from the British Library.

ISBN 0-7445-4172-7

Contents

CHAPTER 1

Bumping into Bato

They treat me like a slave round here.

"Corrina, come and clean this up! Corrina, the kitchen needs sweeping! Do this! Do that! Now, Corrina! *Now!*"

I can't complain, though. I can't complain because I *am* a slave – a slave in a Roman villa – and slaves don't complain. Especially worthless ones like me. You just do your work and keep quiet about it. So when I nearly bumped into Bato, I thought I was in for trouble.

Bumping into Bato's a bad thing to do because Bato's so bossy. He's in charge of all the slaves round here, and he likes everyone to *know* he's in charge.

It happened like this. I dashed into the courtyard and bumped into Bato. I didn't quite bump into him – which was a good thing. I stopped suddenly – which was not a good thing because I was carrying a bucket of slops for the pigs at the time. Bato isn't keen on slops. Especially slops that slop over his sandals and stick between his toes.

I looked down at the puddle of last night's cold gravy dripping over Bato's feet and closed my eyes. The most worthless slave, bumping into the most important servant. He'll be going red in the face and working himself into a temper, I thought. I held my breath and waited.

"Mind out of the *way*, Corrina."

That's all he said. No shouting or beating. Nothing. When I opened my eyes, I saw him hurrying off to the master's rooms on the opposite side of the courtyard. He stopped for a moment to wash his feet at the fishpond by the fountain.

Well, well, well, I thought, there's something going on here.

If ever I want to know what's going on, I take my broom and have a sweep around the place. Nobody notices you if you're busy sweeping. You can sweep right up to people and they don't even see you. So I got my broom and swept across the courtyard, through the doors to the master's quarters and up the stairs. I slowed down outside the bedroom and peered through the keyhole.

There was our master, Aponius Saturninus, still fast asleep on his couch. His lips were flapping as he breathed in and out. Aponius is one of those roly-poly Romans. He likes eating and sleeping and a quiet life. Bato bosses him around, too. He was standing over Aponius and shaking him.

"Master! Wake up, master."

Aponius gave a sort of snort, but he didn't wake up so Bato prodded him in the belly. His finger disappeared in a balloon of fat and Aponius sat up. That shocked me – to prod your own master in the belly! I'd be clapped in chains if I did that.

"Are you prodding me, Bato?" asked Aponius.

"No, master. I think a fly just landed on you. A very big fly. But you ought to be up anyway, master. You'll be late for the sale."

"Sale? What sale?" said Aponius, sinking back on to the couch.

"The Emperor's sale, master. He's selling slaves in Rome today, remember?"

As soon as Bato mentioned the Emperor, Aponius leapt to his feet. One moment he was half-asleep on his couch, and the next he was standing beside it with his eyes wide open and his chins wobbling.

"The *Emperor*, Bato?" he said in a panicky whisper. "The Emperor's sale? Why didn't you tell me? He'll throw me to the lions if I'm late!"

He was running in small circles, trying to find a clean toga and a comb. Crafty old Bato had them all ready for him. He handed Aponius one end of the toga and Aponius began to wrap himself up in it. He was in such a rush that he ended up looking like a finger in a bandage.

"Bato! Bato! I can't move my arms!"

Bato helped him unwind and pushed him to the door, so I grabbed my broom and jumped aside.

"Hurry, master," Bato said. "The chariot's waiting and if we leave now we can still make it."

Well, Bato is keen to get to this sale, I thought. I wonder what he's up to.

Later that evening I heard the familiar clip-clop of the horses coming back through the gates. Off I rushed to get my broom. In came the horses, nodding between the shafts, with Bato looking very smug and jolly and whistling as he flicked the reins. Beside him sat Aponius, his arms folded, not looking at all jolly. Bato jumped down and handed me the reins.

"Hold these a moment, Corrina," he said, "there's a good girl."

A good girl? Me? He *was* feeling pleased with himself.

Aponius's huge backside swung out of the

cart just above my head and I stood smartly out of the way.

"This is all your fault, Bato," Aponius grumbled over his shoulder. "I fell asleep at that sale and you should've woken me up."

"I didn't know you were asleep, master."

"Of course I was asleep. I always fall asleep when it's sunny."

"Ah well, master. I don't think the Emperor really noticed, so no harm done."

"No harm done, Bato? No harm done? Don't you realize that *while* I was asleep I spent fifty gold pieces? Without even knowing it."

"It must be because you were nodding, master," said Bato with a secret smile. "Every time the Emperor asked for a bid, you nodded…"

"I know, I know."

"It's lucky really, master."

"Lucky? Pah!"

"If the Emperor thought you were asleep, he might've thrown you in prison."

The master groaned and looked as if he wanted to do something nasty to Bato. Instead he hit the side of the chariot.

"And look what I've ended up with," he said bitterly. "Just look at them."

I put my nose over the edge of the chariot and looked. Dumped on a pile of straw at the back were two faces sticking out of two coils of thick rope. One had red hair and was scowling and the other was grinning. They were both grubby as pigs.

"Britons!" said Aponius with disgust. "Two dirty, daft-looking Britons. What am I going to do with them?"

"Ah," said Bato smoothly. "I've been thinking about that."

"Don't tell me, Bato," Aponius said. "I don't want to know what you've been thinking." And he stalked off in a huff.

Of course, *I did* want to know, but it was no good asking Bato. He wouldn't tell a worthless slave like me.

CHAPTER 2

Flamma and Diodorus

I took another look at the two new slaves but
that didn't tell me much. One was still
grinning and the other still scowling. When
they spoke, though, I did learn something.
They could speak Latin, but only just.

"Hello," said the grinning one. "Who're
you?"

"Corrina," I said.

"Ooh, nice name. Is this our new home,
Corrina? It looks *lovely*..."

"Hey, Diodorus," the scowling one
scowled. "Why so stupid? You and me are
slaves. We haven't got a home."

"And why so grumpy, Flamma? We're
lucky, really."

They didn't say any more because Bato
joggled the chariot and tipped them out. He
put his foot on them, one after the other, and

rolled them towards the slave quarters.

"Ow-wow-wow-wow!" yelled Flamma, the scowling one. "We can wal-wal-walk, mister!"

Bato took no notice but rolled them into a room which had a window high in one wall and a couple of wooden stools for furniture. There was a pile of straw for a bed, and a wavery pong coming from the straw.

"I'm going to take the ropes off now," Bato told them.

"Thanks, mister," said Diodorus, looking round the room while Bato fiddled with knots. "Cosy place, this."

"Hey!" said Flamma. "Why haven't we got a door?"

"You won't need a door," Bato muttered. "When the main gates are locked no one can get in or out, and if you even *try* to run away, we'll be after you in a flash, and bring you back. In messy little pieces."

He smiled at Flamma and turned to leave.

"One more moment, mate," Diodorus called after him. "I'm not complaining – it's a lovely room, this – but the floor's a bit untidy and…"

Bato took a deep breath and turned round.

"A bit untidy?" he repeated crossly.

"Yes, mate. Someone's left an old crust lying about."

"That's not an old crust," said Bato with a sigh. "It's your *dinner*. And I am *not* your mate. You're slaves, I'm your boss, and I've got some interesting plans for you," he added, wiggling his eyebrows up and down.

"Great, mate. What plans?"

"I'll tell you later."

With that, Bato gave a short, harsh laugh and, as he left, he started whistling again.

"Nice bloke," Diodorus said with a smile at Flamma, who scowled back.

Once Bato had gone, they told me all about themselves. Flamma was short and square, and Diodorus was tall and thin. They were from Briton, which is famous for its terrible weather and for being far away and nothing much else. There they looked after the village pigs. One day they were trying to teach the chief's pig to dance, when it slipped away and ran off. They chased after it and ran straight into a troop of Roman soldiers. So one moment they were free pig-trainers, and the next, Roman slaves with their hands and feet chained. The soldiers gave them Roman names – Flamma, because of his red hair, and Diodorus, because, even though they scrubbed him down, they couldn't get rid of the smell of pigs. They were sold from place to place and ended up in Rome for the Emperor's sale.

"We picked up a bit of Latin on the way," Diodorus said, "and now we're pretty good at talking it."

"So who're you?" Flamma asked.

I told them I was a slave, too, the most worthless slave belonging to Aponius Saturninus.

"Not now," said Diodorus with a wink. "I reckon we're more worthless now."

It was kind of him to say so, but he was

wrong. I found that out in the evening, when Bato looked into the hut again and gave them one of his sickly smiles.

"All settled, lads?" he said. "Good, because it's time to hear my plan."

They looked up at him with eager faces.

"I am going to turn you fine young lads," Bato said slowly, "into gladiators. What do you think of that?"

"Wow!" said Diodorus, clapping his hands. "Gladiators, eh? Thank you, mister. Cheers!"

Bato actually laughed, and you don't see him do that much. We could still hear him chuckling as he made his way across the courtyard to the master's quarters.

"Why so happy about it?" Flamma asked Diodorus when he'd gone. "Do you know what a gladiator is, you *clod-pole*?"

"No. What?"

"I don't know, but I don't like the sound of it."

They turned to me with questioning faces.

"Do you know?" Flamma asked.

Well, of course I knew what gladiators were. I didn't like to come straight out with it, though, so I fiddled around with my broom and tried to think of a way of breaking it to them gently.

"Gladiators?" I said. "Well, they're sort of entertainers."

"Ooh," said Diodorus. "Sounds like fun."

"What do they do, these gladiators?" asked Flamma.

He picked up the crust and tried to chip bits off with a stone.

"They fight," I explained, trying not to look at them. "In a ring with people watching. They fight animals or other gladiators. That sort of thing."

"Hey, that's not fair," said Diodorus. "Poor little animals being hurt."

"The animals don't always get hurt," I said. "And they're not little."

"Well that *is* good."

"Because they're usually wild bears or lions…"

"Lions!" said Diodorus.

"Yes, so sometimes the animals win."

I stopped sweeping and looked at them. Their faces had turned quite white, and they were sitting in the straw staring at each other out of large, round eyes. For the first time since he'd arrived, Diodorus stopped smiling.

"The animals sometimes win," Flamma repeated quietly. "We're going to fight lions and we're going to get *killed*."

"Maybe he didn't say gladiators," Diodorus said. "Maybe he said ... *radiators*."

"Don't be so stupid. There's no such thing as a radiator."

They sat in silence for several minutes. Flamma fiddled with bits of straw and Diodorus sat tapping two bits of crust on the ground between his feet. After a while he began to make one bit growl and jump up and down on the other one.

"Will you stop that?" said Flamma.

"Sorry."

I know they were only a couple of mucky

Britons, but I couldn't help feeling sorry for them.

"Don't worry," I said. "Maybe you'll turn out to be very good gladiators."

"No chance," sighed Diodorus. "You see, we've never gladded before."

He was right, of course. You only had to look at them to know they'd be useless as gladiators. It didn't seem fair – to come all this way just to be beaten to a pulp in a Roman circus, or chewed to a sticky mash by some lion.

Perhaps there's something I can do to help, I thought.

There was. Next morning I took Aponius his breakfast. In my experience, there's nothing like a pile of warm and tasty grub to put him in a good mood. He was still rubbing his eyes and yawning when I set out olives and hot bread and several different kinds of pastry in front of him.

"Lovely morning, master," I said in my

sweetest voice.

"Hmm," said Aponius, pulling the bread apart and taking a good sniff.

He wasn't really listening. Well, he doesn't listen much if there's food about.

"Bato tells me you've bought a couple of gladiators, master."

"Hmm. Excellent bread this morning, Corrina. Tell the kitchens I said so."

He poked a pastry in his mouth and slumped back on his couch. I poured him some wine.

"Hmm. Hmm-hm-hmm!"

(That's Aponius, eating and drinking at the same time.)

"It's a pity to lose them, though, master," I said.

"Hmm?"

"Flamma and Diodorus. The new slaves."

"Why?" Aponius asked in a spray of crumbs.

"Well, master," I said. "I was thinking about the pies."

"Pies?"

Aponius sat up and showed some interest.

"Flamma bakes wonderful pies," I told him, "with thick, golden crusts and succulent, juicy fillings."

"Really?"

Aponius began to dribble.

"And Diodorus – the other one – has magic in his fingers."

"Magic?"

Aponius blinked.

"Yes, he's skilled at massage, master," I continued. "If you've been massaged by Diodorus, they say you feel so relaxed ... so peaceful ... so dreamy..."

But I must've overdone it because Aponius nodded off. I was about to shake him awake when an excited Bato came rushing in with a couple of scrolls.

"I've worked it all out, master," he said. "The cost of training, the profits from the shows..."

He stopped and looked down at the

snoring Aponius.

"Lazy swine," he said. "We're about to launch our very own gladiator school and he falls fast asleep."

He gave the couch a hefty kick and Aponius spluttered and woke up.

"What? What was that?"

"Nothing, master," said Bato. "A small earthquake far away, that's all."

"Oh, dear," said Aponius. "I think I dropped off."

A look of panic crossed his face.

"Bato, I didn't buy any more slaves in my sleep, did I?"

"No, master."

"Good, because Flamma and Diodorus are all I want at the moment."

"Quite so, master," said Bato, turning on a smile so smarmy that I was nearly sick in the wine jug. "And I've just worked out what we'll need to turn them into gladiators..."

"Gladiators? Oh, no, Bato."

"No?"

"No, Flamma and Diodorus aren't going to be gladiators. They're going to be house slaves."

CHAPTER 3

Pour, Slap, Scrape

....

"I knew it," beamed Diodorus when I told them. "I knew the master was nice!"

"But *why*?" asked Flamma. "Why aren't we being gladiators?"

"Ah," I said. "Thanks to me, Aponius wants you to be house slaves instead."

"Wow!" said Diodorus. "House slaves! Fan-*tastic*! What's a house slave, Corrina?"

So I told them about the baking and the massage.

"Baking stuff? I've never cooked a thing in my life," moaned Flamma. "And anyway, what's massage? What if Diodorus can't do it, and the master gets mad and…"

"All right," I interrupted. "You don't have to be house slaves. You can be gladiators instead."

And I turned my back on them and swept off.

"Hey, please," Diodorus called after me. "We'd *love* to be house slaves, Corrina, and I bet we'll be brilliant at it. Whatever it is."

I wasn't so sure about that, but I didn't say anything.

Diodorus started work later that morning in the master's bathroom.

"Listen carefully," I told him. "Aponius stretches out, face down, on this marble slab."

"This marble slab," said Diodorus, nodding.

"Then you pour some oil on his back and rub it in."

He gave me a puzzled look.

"You're sure you've got this right?" he said. "Flamma's doing the cooking."

"This is not cooking, you fool. This is massage!"

"No need to shout, Corrina. I only asked."

"Yes, all right. I'm sorry."

"So I don't put him in any oven or anything?"

"No, no, no! Massage, not cooking! You rub the oil in and then you get this scraper and scrape it off."

"I rub it in, and then scrape it off?" said Diodorus, looking even more puzzled.

"Be careful, though. You have to be firm but gentle."

"Firm but gentle. Right."

The master came plodding in, wrapped in a sheet. He paused a moment and sniffed.

"Do I smell pigs?" he asked.

"You do," said Diodorus. "And isn't it sweet?"

"No, it isn't," said Aponius.

He flopped on to the marble slab, took a deep breath and closed his eyes. And waited. Nothing happened.

"Get on with it, then," I whispered.

Diodorus was staring down at the master's vast, flabby buttocks. He bit his lip and his eyes filled with tears.

"What's the matter now?"

"I'm thinking of home, Corrina," he

sniffed. "There were two big hills outside the village and..."

"These aren't hills; they're buttocks, Diodorus," I told him, and handed him the oil. "Just get on with it."

Aponius lay there, completely still, snoring gently.

"Pour, slap, scrape," Diodorus muttered to himself. "Pour, scrape, slap... No, no. Slap, scrape, pour..."

He was in such a state of nerves he almost tipped the oil all over the sheet.

"No," I hissed, just managing to snatch it away from him. "You have to take the sheet off first."

"But he's got no clothes on," he said, his eyes round with shock.

"Of course he hasn't!"

"But, Corrina, that's *rude*."

"You have to rub the oil into his skin!"

"All right, all right," said Diodorus shortly. "Don't get bossy."

"You dolt!"

I suppose I shouldn't have said that. I suppose I should've been more patient. Diodorus looked stung.

"I know what I'm doing," he said, and he grabbed the sheet.

He gave it a firm tug and sent Aponius spinning off the edge of the slab. There was a thud and a groan. Two or three seconds passed before a pale face appeared, blinking, on the other side of the slab.

"Magic fingers?" Aponius said in a soft, pained voice. "Peaceful and dreamy?"

"That's only the first move, master," Diodorus stammered. "From now on it gets a lot more peaceful."

"Get out!" bellowed the master. "Get out, the pair of you!"

But we were already on our way.

While Diodorus spent the afternoon hiding under a pile of straw, I took Flamma to the kitchens to prepare a pie. He wasn't very happy about it. He said the kitchens were hot

and steamy, and he thought he'd get a
headache, and the cooks looked bad-
tempered and awkward, and...

"Don't moan," I told him. "It's better to
bake a pie than to be killed by a lion, isn't it?"

"Better still to stay at home and look after
pigs," Flamma moaned.

There wasn't time to argue about it,
though. He had a succulent pie to bake by
four o'clock. Then he had to put the pie on a
dish, a smile on his face, and take it to the
master.

"Do I *have* to smile?" Flamma asked.

"Yes," I snapped, and I flashed my teeth to
show him what a smile looked like.

Flamma did his best – I'm sure he did his
best – but he didn't have much flair with
food. In fact, he was hopeless. *Really*
hopeless. He couldn't even keep the pastry
on the table. I showed him how to roll it out,
but when he tried, it kept flipping to the floor.
Every time he picked it up, it had more hairs
and twigs and bits of grit stuck to it, but he

just poked them into the pastry and rolled it out again. Soon it was looking all grey and streaky, more like wet sand than pastry.

"Keep it on the table, Flamma," I said.

"I'm trying to," he answered, "but *he* keeps putting me off."

He nodded in the direction of the window where a scruffy-looking dog was staring in at us. His paws were resting on the window ledge and he seemed to be fascinated by Flamma's efforts. It was Scrag. Scrag was always hanging around the villa, scrounging for scraps and grubbing about in all the filth he could find. He loved muck, Scrag did, so much so that he actually looked like it – muck on legs.

"It's only Scrag," I said. "Take no notice."

"I can't, Corrina. With dogs staring at me. Clear off!"

Suddenly he picked up the pastry and flung it at the window. It sailed through the air and wrapped itself round Scrag's face. Scrag gave a muffled yelp and fell backwards into the courtyard. We dashed outside and chased him round and round in circles while he tried to lick the pastry off his face. By the time we caught him, it was covered in slobber and something sticky and unpleasant that Scrag had been chewing half an hour before.

"Now what are we going to do?" I said. "It's nearly four o'clock already."

"Pop it in the oven," Flamma said nervously. "Maybe it'll look nice and tasty when it's cooked."

CHAPTER 4

Good News/Bad News

··

"Do you want the good news or the bad news?" Bato said, beaming at them from ear to ear.

It wasn't a pretty sight.

"Good news, mate," said Diodorus.

"Bad news first," chipped in Flamma.

Their wrists and feet were chained and they were sitting back to back on their pile of straw. Bato paced up and down in front of them with a large scroll tucked under his arm. Every so often he bopped one of them on the head with it. He was enjoying himself no end.

"I'm afraid that Aponius Saturninus is in a poor way," he said. "He's covered with bruises from his relaxing massage."

BOP! on Diodorus's head.

"And the succulent pie made him violently sick."

BOP! on Flamma's head.

"He shouldn't have eaten it, then," grumbled Flamma.

"He didn't…"

BOP!

"He was sick just looking at it."

BOP!

"So what's the bad news?" Flamma asked.

"Ha…"

BOP!

"Ha!"

BOP!

"The *good* news is that he's decided not to have you chopped into little pieces and fed to rats. He's going to give you another chance."

Oh, dear, I thought. I know what this means.

"He's going to try you out as gladiators after all," said Bato. "Won't that be fun?"

"What do you mean 'try us out'?" Diodorus asked.

"It's quite simple, my gormless friend. One of you is going to fight a wild beast. If you do well, the master will start a *ludi*."

"A what?"

"A *ludi*. A gladiator school."

"And if we do badly..." said Flamma.

"You'll be chopped into little pieces..."

BOP!

"...and fed to rats."

BOP! BOP!

Bato smiled happily and tossed a coin to decide who would be Aponius's first gladiator.

"Heads!" called Diodorus.

Heads it was.

"Hooray!" he cried.

But winning the toss meant he was the one who'd have to face the wild beast.

The courtyard was prepared. The main gates were locked and all doors were barred so that the wild and savage beast Diodorus had to fight couldn't get indoors to eat anyone. Of course, if you happened to be in the courtyard, you couldn't get indoors either.

Diodorus pointed this out to Bato.

"But you won't *want* to get indoors," Bato said soothingly. "You'll want to be out there struggling with the wild and savage beast, won't you?"

"Not much, no," mumbled Diodorus and he dragged himself off to get ready for battle.

He was making for the kitchens and he looked a sorry sight, his face pale green and his shoulders hunched. He tried to smile but it wasn't very convincing. Smiles don't really work if your face is green.

"Why is he going to the kitchens?" Flamma asked.

"To get something to eat, I expect," said Bato. "After all, it could be his last meal."

Bato, Flamma and I went along to the master's dining room with a jug of wine and two trays of buns so that Aponius would have something to nibble while he watched. We found him sitting at the window, out of harm's way and looking peckish. In fact, there were faces at all the windows which overlooked the courtyard. Everyone in the villa knew about the great contest – the spindly young Briton against a wild and savage beast – and no one wanted to miss it.

"You see?" Bato whispered smugly. "Gladiator contests are *extremely* popular. The master could make a lot of money out of this."

"You could, you mean," I muttered.

"I might make a little bit, Corrina," he chuckled. "Where's the harm in that?"

There was a shout outside and we crowded to the window. We saw someone push Diodorus out of the kitchens and slam the door behind him. He was armed with a toasting fork and had two dishes strapped to him, one on his head and one on his chest.

"So that's why he went to the kitchens," I said.

He must've been in a hurry because the dish on his head hadn't been washed up properly. Dribbles of fish sauce were running down his cheeks. He tried to wipe them away with the back of his hand, but that made him stumble and roll over on his back like a tired tortoise.

"I say!" said Aponius suddenly. "That's the boy who knocked me off the table. What's he doing out there?"

"He's your new gladiator, master," explained Bato.

"Why is he covered in dishes?"

"To protect himself. Against the wild beast."

"What wild beast, Bato? What are you talking about? This is ridiculous. That poor boy can hardly stand up. If he's not careful, he's going to break my dishes. And then what'll they cook my dinner in?"

There was a sudden commotion across the courtyard, and another door – the door to the stables – was flung open. All the onlookers sucked in their breath.

"Get up, Dio!" Flamma yelled, so loud that Aponius gave a little jump and dropped the bun that was halfway to his mouth. "The beastie's coming!"

Diodorus struggled to his feet, tilted the sauce-dish so he could see, and staggered back. From the darkness of the stables, the beast lurched slowly into the courtyard.

It was disgusting.

Something black and sticky dripped from its jaws.

It lowered its filthy head.

It wagged its tail.

Wagged its tail?

"Just a minute," I said. "That's not a wild and savage beast. That's Scrag!"

"Well," Bato said out of the corner of his mouth, "I won't make much money if my gladiator gets eaten in his first fight, will I?"

Out in the courtyard, Scrag scampered up to Diodorus and bounced him over with his front paws. I think he'd caught a whiff of the fish sauce. Or maybe pigs.

"By Jove!" cried Bato in the master's ear. "Look at that! He's really wild! He's dangerous and violent!"

"Oh, the poor boy!" said Aponius, leaning on the window ledge and chewing his fingers. "He's being *savaged*!"

Actually, Scrag was licking his face. And Diodorus was laughing as he tried to push him off.

"Just listen to his cries of terror, master," Bato said.

"I can't bear it! I can't bear it!" whimpered Aponius, and he hid his face in his hands. "Call the brute off!"

"There's no stopping him now, I'm afraid."

Meanwhile, Diodorus had wriggled free and Scrag was bouncing about, yapping and thrashing his tail from side to side. I'd never seen him enjoy himself so much. Diodorus grabbed hold of the edge of the fountain and pulled himself to his knees. He waved an arm as the dog made another lunge, and water splashed everywhere. Scrag sprang back and blinked. You could see what he was thinking: Oh no, I'm being washed.

"Look, master!" shouted Bato. "The brave

gladiator's fighting back!"

Aponius peered through his fingers and saw Diodorus chasing Scrag round the courtyard and flicking water at him. He was yelping with the excitement of it all. So was Scrag. Twice round the courtyard they raced, and then the dog bolted into the stables and the boy slammed the door on him. A great cheer went up from all the windows.

"Great Jove and Juno," breathed Bato, wiping pretend sweat from his brow. "Have you ever seen anything so *thrilling*, master?"

Aponius slumped back in his chair and puffed out his cheeks.

"Never, Bato," he said. "Never in my life. When can I see some more?"

"Soon, master," Bato answered.

Then he turned and gave the thumbs-up sign to Flamma and me. His grin was so wide that the sun flashed off his teeth.

CHAPTER 5

Verus

The *Ludi* Aponius Saturninus, they called it:
Aponius's school for gladiators. It wasn't a
very big school. There were only three people
in it – Flamma and Diodorus, and an ex-
gladiator called Verus, hired by Bato to be
their teacher.

Verus was hard. He had a face like a piece
of worn leather screwed into a tight ball. Bato
was delighted with him, but he looked to me
as if he'd been chewed by wild animals and
then spat out because he was too tough.

"Ah," said Bato with a wink, "that's
because he has."

Well, I didn't believe it so I asked Verus
himself. He spent the next hour telling me
how a lion grabbed him when he wasn't
looking and attempted to chomp him up.

"Spat me out in the end," he growled.

"Too tough for lions, girl. That's me."

He was very proud of that.

Work at the school began with an inspection for Flamma and Diodorus. Verus walked up and down in front of them for several minutes without saying a word. I don't think he was very impressed.

"You dis-*gusting* little people!" he barked into their faces. "What do they call shorty, here?"

"Flamma," said Diodorus, trying to be helpful.

"And what do they call lanky, here?"

"Diodorus," said Flamma.

"Step out here, Flamma!" Verus screamed.

Diodorus took a sharp step forward.

"Not you, not you! You pile of mouse droppings, you! I said FLAMMA!"

"Oh dearie me," said Diodorus with a little laugh, "you've blundered there, Verus. You see, you asked what he's called and so I said…"

"SHUT UP!"

"I'm only trying to help…"

"Shut your 'orrible face UP!!"

Diodorus shut up.

"Now," snarled Verus, "I've been eaten by a lion so don't muck me about. Which of you nasty animals is which?"

"Easy to tell," said Diodorus, still trying to be helpful. "That's Flamma. He's short, see, and he's got a short name. Just remember 'short', mate, and you can…"

"I want an answer, not a bloomin' CONVERSATION! From now on I don't CARE what your lousy names are. I shall call you Tall and Short. Right?"

Diodorus had a question and he put his finger in the air.

"What?" snapped Verus.

"Which one are you calling Short and which one—"

"WHAARGH-orrah-INNIT!!" yelled Verus, so loud that it made a couple of dishes on the kitchen window ledge rattle.

I don't know what it meant exactly, but I

sort of guessed. So did Diodorus and Flamma, because they didn't ask any more questions. They just stood to attention and tried not to shake.

The first lesson was what Verus called "non-flinching practice". He told them that to be a gladiator you have to be brave and steady. A gladiator never flinches. A gladiator never even *blinks*.

"Now then," said Verus, "I'm going to make a sudden movement, and I want you two animals to stand firm. I *don't* want you to flinch, and I *don't* want you to blink. Right?"

"Right," said Diodorus and Flamma.

Verus put his hand to his side and drew his sword.

They blinked.

They flinched.

In fact, Flamma fell flat on his face and Diodorus ran to hide behind the fountain.

"That was USELESS! That was TERRIBLE! Get back here NOW!"

They crept back and Verus tried again.

This time they flinched as soon as his hand twitched.

"Don't MOVE!" he roared. "*I* didn't flinch when I was being eaten by a lion. Don't *you* flinch just because I twiddle my fingers, you pair of JELLIES!"

So on and on they went, Verus going for his sword and the boys standing as stiff as posts and trying not to blink. They couldn't help it, though. After half an hour their eyes were still fluttering away like butterflies, and Verus decided to move on to lesson two: the gladiator's salute.

"I am now going to teach you what to do at the START of a FIGHT," he announced.

"Thank goodness for that," sighed Diodorus. "My nerves are in shreds."

"No talking in the RANKS! Now then, THIS is what you do: you march smartly to the CENTRE of the ring. You turn to where all the most important people are sitting, and you give THIS salute."

Stamping one foot, Verus bashed himself

on the chest with his fist.

"Dead easy, see. RIGHT, Tall, you try first."

So Diodorus stamped one foot and tapped his chest.

"No, no, NO! Hit your chest HARD! Hit it!"

"I'll hurt myself if I do," said Diodorus.

"Hurt? You wibbly-wobbly WEAKLING. When you've been eaten by a lion you can talk to me about being hurt. Short, you try it."

"Does it have to be my chest?" Flamma asked. "Because I've got a bit of a cough and—"

"Whack your chest NOW, or I'll whack it for you!"

So Flamma whacked his chest, and immediately started coughing. He coughed so much that Diodorus had to slap his back. Verus turned away from them, holding his hand to his brow like a man with a sudden headache.

"All right, all right," he said after a moment's thought. "Let's do it AGAIN, and this time get it RIGHT!"

They did it another twenty times or so, with Verus shouting, "March, march. Stamp, stamp. BASH!" until Diodorus and Flamma had almost knocked themselves out. Still, they got it more or less right in the end. They had no time to feel pleased, though, because then they had to learn the gladiator's chant.

"When you make the SALUTE," Verus barked, "you shout out, 'We who are about to die salute you!'"

"What was that?" said Flamma, looking appalled. "We who are *about to die*?"

"That's what I said."

"But that's a terrible thing to say."

"I don't care. ALL gladiators have to say it."

"No, no, mister. We can't talk about *dying*," Flamma said.

"I know," suggested Diodorus. "Why don't we say, 'We who are about to put on a show, salute you'?"

Verus went red in the face and glared at him.

"Because it's a SOFT thing to say, you WORM!" he said. "People have to know that gladiators face REAL DANGER."

"Then how about 'We who are about to *fall over*, salute you'?" Diodorus offered.

"No, no, NO!" yelled Verus, stamping his foot. "Just do what I SAY, will you?"

By the end of the day he was looking even more worn out and fed up than they were. In fact, he looked as if he'd *rather* be eaten by a lion than teach Flamma and Diodorus how to be gladiators.

CHAPTER 6

Show Time

....

Every day for the next few weeks, I sneaked
out to watch the training. Diodorus and
Flamma did improve a little, I suppose, but
Verus got steadily worse. And even more bad-
tempered. Try as he might, he couldn't make
them FIERCE enough. Once Diodorus
accidentally poked Flamma with his wooden
practice sword, and dropped it at once to see
if his friend was all right.

"No, no, NO!" Verus bellowed. "You've got
to be ruthless. You've got to get in there and
JAB HIM!"

"I can't do that," Diodorus said. "What if
he gets a splinter or something? Anyway, he's
my mate, mate."

And he pulled Flamma to his feet.

Verus was tough all right – as hard as a
centurion's helmet – but those two were

wearing him to a frazzle.

Once or twice Aponius wandered out to the courtyard to watch. He stared at them for a while and then wandered in again to comfort himself with a plate of buns. The excitement of the fight with Scrag had worn off. I think he was bored with the *Ludi* Aponius Saturninus.

"The trouble is," I heard him say to Bato one day over breakfast, "I'm paying for their food and all they do is *play*."

"It's not play, master, it's training," said Bato. "And they're nearly ready for their first big show."

"But if I sold them I could afford more food or something."

"Well, master, if you want to tell Verus you've changed your mind…"

Which was a clever thing to say. We all glanced out of the window into the courtyard, where we could see Verus demonstrating a few cuts with the sword.

"Cut! And THRUST! And SWIPE!" he was

shouting as he jabbed at a sack of straw hanging from a rope.

He was blazing with rage and energy, and the straw was flying all over the place.

"Couldn't *you* have a word with him, Bato?" Aponius asked.

"Oh, I don't think that would be right, master," Bato said smoothly.

Of course, he knew Aponius was scared of Verus. Well, we all were. He was so *savage*. Say the wrong thing and he'd swipe your head off. Or bore you to death with the story of the man-eating lion, which was probably worse. So Aponius heaved a sigh and went back to his breakfast. He said no more about selling Flamma and Diodorus after that.

In the evenings I used to take the boys their food. They were always pleased to see me, but they weren't quite so pleased to see the food. They were hungry enough, but the food was a horrible, gritty, grey mash. This was because Verus mixed ash with it.

"It'll toughen you UP," he said. "Put fire in

your BELLIES."

"I don't want fire in my belly," Flamma moaned when I gave him his dish. "I just want plain *food*."

"Ah well," said Diodorus, "it's grubby grub all right, but at least we're still alive."

"No thanks to Mister Misery-guts Verus."

"He's not so bad when you're used to him."

(That was just like Diodorus. He was the only one in the whole villa who thought that.)

"I don't *want* to get used to him," Flamma said. "And if I hear about him getting eaten by a lion once more, I'll go screaming up the wall."

"Well, I quite *like* being a gladiator," said Diodorus with a chuckle, and he began to sing a little song as he stirred his food. "*Oh, I'm glad, glad to be a glad, pom-pom-pom!*" – until Flamma flicked a dollop of ash mash at him, catching him square on the end of his nose.

Deep down, I think Flamma agreed with

Diodorus. True, they *were* slaves, and they *were* far from home, but it could have been worse. I pointed this out, and Flamma asked me *how* it could be worse. Then Bato came humming round the corner, and we found out.

"Having fun, lads?" he smirked at them.

"Oh, hello there, matey," said Diodorus, picking mash off the end of his nose. "I was just making up a little song. Would you like to hear it?"

"I'd *love* to hear it, my quaint friend."

I knew they were in for trouble when Bato said that. You can never trust a man like Bato when he gets all smarmy. Diodorus trusted everyone though, so he took a breath and sang his song for the slimy toad.

"Oh, I'm glad, glad to be a glad, pom-pom-pom! Yes, I'm glad, so glad to be a glad, diddle-iddle-om!"

He was making it up as he went along and it was pretty dreadful. I trod on Scrag's tail once by accident, and the row he made

sounded much sweeter than Diodorus's song.
Even so, Bato hummed along and pretended
to like it.

"I'm glad you're glad, Diodorus," he said.
"And soon you can show us all just how glad
you are."

"What do you mean by that?" asked
Flamma.

"I mean it's show time!"

"Show time!" said Diodorus. "Lovely. I can
sing my song and Flamma can do a little
dance…"

Bato laughed and shook his head.

"No, no," he said. "I mean a *gladiator* show.
I've arranged your first real fight."

Everything went quiet and I heard Flamma
swallow.

"With Scrag?" said Diodorus. "That's nice,
except he sometimes slobbers all over you
and…"

"No. Not Scrag," said Bato, still smiling.
"Oh?"

"You see, there's a very rich Roman family

on the next estate, and they're having a
wedding."

"Well, that's nice."

"Yes, Diodorus. It *is* nice. Very nice. And
you're going to be the entertainment."

"Wow! We'd love that, wouldn't we
Flamma?"

"Oh, yes," Bato went on. "A wedding
needs a good fight with plenty of biffing and
bashing and buckets of blood..."

"A fight?" I said slowly. "You mean ... lions
and things?"

"No, Corrina, not lions. Lions are *so*
expensive. I've thought of something much
cheaper than that."

What's cheaper than lions? I thought. And
why does he look so jolly?

"You're wondering what's cheaper than
lions," Bato said. "Well, gladiators are
cheaper than lions."

"Gladiators?" Flamma repeated.

"That's right. You're going to fight each other."

As he walked out into the courtyard, Bato

began to sing Diodorus's little tune.

"*Oh, I'm glad, glad to be a glad, pom-pom-pom…*"

When he'd gone, I turned to Flamma and Diodorus with a glum face, and found they were both smiling. I couldn't believe it.

"Phew!" said Diodorus with a little laugh. "I thought we were in real trouble just then."

They thought it was all a joke. Obviously they didn't know about the way things are done in Rome.

"Don't you understand?" I said. "You have to fight each other."

"That's all right," said Flamma. "We can *pretend* to fight, can't we?"

"No, you can't. People don't want pretend fights. They want one of you to win. They want one of you to smash the other one up. And if you don't, they'll do you both in."

"They won't," said Diodorus. "Will they?"

"Yes! It has to be a real fight, with real bashing and real blood."

"No, no," Flamma said firmly. "They can't make me smash Diodorus up."

"Oh yes they can. You're slaves, remember."

Diodorus tapped Flamma on the chest with his finger.

"Hang on," he said. "Who says you'll smash me up? I might smash *you* up."

"Don't argue," I said. "That won't get you anywhere."

"Then what are we going to do?" asked Flamma.

I had no answer to that. Neither did Diodorus. We sat in the gloom for a while, staring at the floor. Then Diodorus looked up and clapped his hands together.

"I've got it!" he piped.

"What?"

"We can go on strike."

I didn't know what he was talking about. Strike? The only kind of striking gladiators did was with swords and clubs and things.

"No, no," he explained. "A strike is when you refuse to work. If a thing's not fair, you down tools."

"Down tools?"

"Yes. You put your tools down."

"Oh, that's clever, mate," snorted Flamma. "And what *are* your tools?"

"Well, you know: that swordy-thing or a club…"

"So you put them down and then what?"

"Verus will just walk up to you and WHACK!" I said.

"Hmm. Good point."

So then we were back to staring at the floor.

CHAPTER 7

Plots and Plans

For the next couple of days we nearly wore our brains out trying to work out what to do. And we got nowhere. Diodorus was the only one to come up with any ideas, but they were all pretty daft. One of them was pretend blood. He said they should get some berry juice and splash it all over themselves.

"And what do we do about the broken bones?" said Flamma. "How do we do that?"

"We get sticks, and hide them in our tunics," Diodorus said enthusiastically. "And then we snap them, and we yell, 'Ow! Argh! That really hurts!'"

I wanted to know what would happen when Verus came to carry the bodies away. He'd find two healthy gladiators on a pile of snapped sticks and squashed berries. Then there'd be some real blood and a few real broken bones.

"Hmm. You've got a point there, Corrina," he said.

At least he was trying, though. And in the end he was the one who came up with the best plan, though he did it by accident. It came about when Scrag sneaked into their room and helped himself to their ash mash. This was the last straw for Diodorus. He suddenly stopped being bright and cheerful, folded his arms and sulked.

"I wish we'd never come here," he moaned. "I wish we were somewhere else, miles away."

And that reminded me of Spartacus.

"Of course," I said, clicking my fingers. "Spartacus!"

"No need to be rude," grumbled Diodorus.

"I'm not," I said. "Don't you know about Spartacus?"

Being Britons they didn't. So I told them.

"A few years ago there was a gladiator called Spartacus," I began.

"Oh, that's all we need," said Flamma.

"We're about to be *killed* and Corrina comes up with history lessons. Well, thanks for nothing…"

"Stop moaning, Flamma. If you listen you might find a way out of this mess. Now, Spartacus decided he'd had enough of being a gladiator. So what did he do? For a start, he didn't fold his arms and sulk. No, he decided to escape."

"Escape?" said Flamma. "Bato said we'd be chopped up and the rats would eat us if we tried that."

"Yes but Spartacus did try it, and he got away with it. He got all the other gladiators to join him and they formed an army and ran away to Mount Vesuvius. Of course, the Roman army went after them, but Spartacus trained his army of gladiators so well that they actually beat the Roman army in battle after battle."

"What's this got to do with us?"

"It's obvious. You can do the same."

"Yes!" cried Diodorus. "Escape and get up

an army! Wow! What an adventure!"

"One small moment," said Flamma, holding up his hands. "How many gladiators did this Smarty-pus have in his army?"

"Er ... about seventy thousand, I think."

He stroked his chin and did some counting on his fingers.

"Let me see, now. If we get all the gladiators here to join us, we'd have ... two."

"It's a start," I said. "And I could join you."

"No, Corrina. *Your* life isn't in danger."

That was true, and it was good of Flamma to say so, but suddenly I found I wanted to join them. While I was a slave, I was worthless. If I could escape, well, I might become something better. I was fed up with sweeping the villa, backwards and forwards, time after time. But there was another reason for going with them; something that had just occurred to me.

"Anyway," I said. "You need me."

"Why do we need you, Corrina?" asked Diodorus.

"Because, if you get out, you won't know where to go or what to do. You don't know Roman ways and you can't even speak proper Latin."

Flamma didn't like it but he could see I was right. So that made Diodorus, Flamma and me. Three.

"Three doesn't quite make an army," Flamma said.

There was a rustling in the straw and Scrag stuck his head out.

"That's four now," said Diodorus. "You'll join us, won't you, boy?"

And Scrag licked his chops and panted as if he was really keen on the idea.

Two boys, a slave girl and a dog. The Romans weren't going to run away from us in fear of their lives. (They might've run away from Scrag, I suppose, in fear of being slobbered on, but it wasn't quite the same.) Still, there wasn't much choice. Either the boys tried to escape, or they stayed behind and fought each other and ended up in pieces.

After the escape we planned to head for the coast and catch a boat somewhere. It didn't matter where – just somewhere far from Aponius's villa. A town by the sea would be a good place. It would be full of foreigners and the boys' speech wouldn't seem so odd. We all agreed about that. What we couldn't agree about was how we were going to escape. So the boys carried on training, and the day of the show drew nearer and nearer, and we kept thinking.

One sunny afternoon they were taking a break while Verus went off to do some press-ups on his own. Diodorus was leaning against the fountain with his eyes closed, and Flamma was stretched out flat on his back. I took my broom and went sweeping over to them.

"Any ideas?" I asked when I was close enough.

"Yes," said Flamma without moving a muscle. "I've got a brilliant idea."

"What?"

"Let's go to sleep. It's too hot to think."

"Then go to sleep," I said. "And if you wake up on the day of the show, don't blame me."

"I've had a thought, Corrina," said Diodorus. "The problem is the gates. They're always shut, right?"

"Yes."

"So why don't we jump *over* the gates?"

"Because they're twice as high as you are, Diodorus."

"I know, but if I hold my hands together, and Flamma takes a run and steps on them … well, over he springs."

"Not likely," said the motionless Flamma. "I'd land on my head."

"Anyway," I added, "you can only spring two of us like that. How are *you* going to get out?"

"Hmm. I didn't think of that."

"No, we have to *sneak* out somehow, so we can get away before they miss us."

So we sat thinking for a while until a huge cloud passed over the sun and our part of the courtyard suddenly became cool and shadowy.

"Ah," said Diodorus. "A big fat cloud. *Lovely*. Lovely and cool. Oh, hello," he added, gaping up at the cloud, his eyes suddenly round and his mouth opening and shutting like a fish.

I wondered what sort of cloud could make him do that, and I turned round to see. It wasn't any sort of cloud. It was Aponius Saturninus and he was standing right behind us.

"So," Aponius said slowly. "You're planning to sneak out, are you?"

At the sound of his voice Flamma woke up and shot to his feet.

"No, no, master," I stammered. "Not *sneak* out, no..."

"I heard everything you said, Corrina. Don't deny it."

I felt sick. We were caught red-handed,

planning to escape. We'd be chopped up and fed to rats. What could we do? I reached out and tried to kiss the master's fat fingers. They were horribly hot and sticky, but it was worth a try.

"Get off me," Aponius said, pulling his hand away.

"Please," whimpered Diodorus, "I don't really think you're a big, fat cloud."

"Admit it. You were planning to escape."

"Of course not, master," I started to explain, but Aponius interrupted me with something that really took my breath away.

"Why not?" he said.

"Why not?"

"Yes. Why not?"

"Well," said Diodorus, "the gates are too big and they're always locked..."

Flamma jabbed an elbow in his ribs and he stopped. Aponius leaned closer, his round face looming over us like the moon.

"I'll help you if you like," he whispered.

"What?"

"I don't want to watch people bashing each other about, Corrina. I want good food and lots of rest, not violence. So I'll help you escape if you like. If…"

"If what?" asked Flamma.

"You don't breathe a word to Bato or that bully Verus."

CHAPTER 8

Pots and Pans

....

We thought it would be easy with Aponius on our side, but it wasn't. He told us he *wanted* to open the gates – just like that – and send us on our way, but he couldn't do it.

"Why not?" asked Flamma.

"Well," he said vaguely, "it's rather tricky. To do with keys and things, you see. It all has to be planned and plotted..."

He twittered on for some minutes, but I guessed the real reason was that he was scared stiff of Bato and Verus. I didn't blame him. Bato was so slippery, and Verus such a bully. They'd make his life miserable if they knew he'd helped us escape, even though he was the master.

So the plan was that he'd creep out at midnight – I couldn't imagine him creeping, but never mind about that – and unlock the gates for five minutes. When he sneaked back to bed, we'd slip out. Then he'd come tip-toeing back to lock up again. No one would know a thing about it till the morning.

It should've worked like a dream. It *would've* worked like a dream, if Diodorus hadn't had another of his bright ideas. He thought that because we were an army, we should be dressed like an army.

"We'll need armour," he said. "When I fought my mate Scrag, I wore dishes and things. If we do the same we'll be protected."

At the time, it didn't seem a bad idea so we agreed. Just before midnight, there we were, waiting in the shadows by the kitchens, with all sorts of pots and pans tied round us. Even Scrag had a small saucepan strapped to his head. We felt well protected, but every time we made the slightest move we clanked. And that meant we had to tread very slowly and carefully. Big, wide steps. Step and wait, step and wait.

By the time we got out to the courtyard, it

was five past midnight.

And there was something funny about the gates.

"Someone's left a great big bundle of sheets here," whispered Flamma.

It wasn't a bundle of sheets. It was the master in his night-gown. He thought we'd already escaped and he was back to lock up.

"Pst!" called Diodorus. "Aponius Saturninus! Pst!"

The master looked over his shoulder and saw three weird figures glinting in the moonlight and lumbering towards him. His face turned the colour of his night-gown and he began to quiver.

"Oh Jove, help me," he squealed. "Ghosts!"

He fell back against the gates and waved his arms wildly.

"Keep away! Keep away!"

"Ssh!" we hissed. "It's only us."

But the sight of Aponius flailing his arms about was too much for Scrag. He thought it was some new game and he started bouncing up and down and yelping.

"It's the hound of Hades!" cried Aponius. "He's come for me! He's come for me!"

Scrag was delighted. He made a dash for the master, and Flamma made a dash for Scrag. But the pots and pans slowed him down and Scrag had no trouble in darting out of the way. Well, not quite out of the way. He somehow managed to get himself under Flamma's feet, and Flamma toppled over with a mighty crash.

"What's going on out there?" a rough voice shouted from one of the rooms across the courtyard.

A flickering candle appeared at a window.

"Help!" bellowed Aponius. "The hound of Hades is after me!"

"No, master, no," I said, whipping a pudding basin off my head so he could see me. "It's us."

"You? But haven't you already gone?"

"Of course we haven't, you clod," snapped Flamma.

(A slave should never really talk to his master like that, but Flamma was all on edge.)

"All right, all right," said Aponius, and he fumbled with the key to unlock the gates a second time.

I heard the lock click open, but the master was shaking so much that the key jiggled out of his fingers and fell to the ground. As we bundled through, my foot caught it and sent it spinning ahead of us.

"Pick it up, Corrina," said Flamma. "We might need it later."

Once outside, we turned to push the gates shut. There was a deep boom as they closed, and then the sound of heavy footsteps thundering across the courtyard. They were coming fast, and we were going slow – clank, rattle, plod, plod.

"All these dishes," snorted Flamma to Diodorus. "Another stupid idea!"

I heard the swish of a sword and Verus's gruff voice.

"It's Short and Tall!" he cried. "They're escaping! Open those gates!"

And suddenly the night was full of noise – Bato shouting, Verus and Scrag barking, and the gates banging as we all pushed on one side and Verus and Bato on the other.

They're too strong for us, I thought. They'll catch us easily now.

And, sure enough, bit by bit, we were being forced back. A small gap opened and Verus's face appeared in it, his eyes blazing and his cheeks puffed out like a frog's. His arm reached through and he was about to grab Diodorus by the throat when there was a heavy thud and he shot out of sight.

"Wow!" said Diodorus. "What's happening to *him*?"

What happened to him was that Aponius had fallen over and landed on top of him. He was wedged in the gap and we could just see his legs wriggling underneath the master's floundering body.

"Oof! Get this lump off me!" came a

muffled cry.

Bato took hold of Verus's leg and yanked it. "Ow! Ow!"

"I fought them off, Bato," Aponius was shouting. "Did you see me? I was incredibly brave. One of them's a wild beast, and they're all armed and…"

"Get this tub of jelly off my face!" Verus called out from beneath him.

Legs and arms were waving all over the place. Bato, red in the face and gritting his teeth, rolled Aponius off Verus and immediately we felt the gates move. They juddered and shut. I saw my chance, put the key in the lock and gave it a sharp twist. Then I flung it far into the bushes.

"The gates are locked!" yelled Verus. "How can we get at them now?"

Flamma and Diodorus began to take off their kitchen armour and fling it aside. I did the same. We'd have to run for it. No good being done up like a tortoise when you have to run.

"Mind where you put your great flat foot, you oaf!" shouted Aponius on the other side of the gates.

"Careful! You can't tread on the master like that," Bato was saying.

"Stay still and let me get at them!"

Verus must've been trying to climb over Aponius to reach the top of the gates.

"There's no need to climb!" shouted Bato. "I've got a spare key!"

"Where?"

"In my room."

"Then go and get it!"

Bato's footsteps pattered away into the night. There was a moment's silence and then a splash. He'd found the fish-pond.

"Did you see me, Verus?" Aponius was saying in a shaky voice. "Did you see how brave I was? Did you see the fight I put up?"

We didn't wait to hear Verus answer. We threw off the last of the pots and pans and ran into the darkness for all we were worth, with Scrag yapping excitedly at our heels.

Aponius was right in a way. He *had* been brave. And he *had* put up a fight. Of course, he was fighting to help us escape, not to get us back, but Bato and Verus didn't know that.

So, thank you, Aponius Saturninus. May the gods reward you with endless supplies of sticky pastries. You saved our lives.

By the time Bato got back to the gates with the spare key, we were far away, heading for the coast and a boat to freedom. Two mucky Britons and a dog.

And me, because they couldn't have done it without me, Corrina, the most worthless slave in the villa.